For Ashley, Sam, and Tenika, who filled my home and my heart
—A. J.

To librarians everywhere and to Sarah and Sophia—two of the most book-lovin' girls I know!
—S. M. F.

ACKNOWLEDGMENTS
Thanks to team Lottie: Angela J., Laurent, Julia, and Angela D.!
—S. M. F.

SIMON & SCHUSTER BOOKS FOR YOUNG READERS
An imprint of Simon & Schuster Children's Publishing Division
1230 Avenue of the Americas, New York, New York 10020
Text copyright © 2013 by Angela Johnson
Illustrations copyright © 2013 by Scott Fischer
All rights reserved, including the right of reproduction in whole or in part in any form.
SIMON & SCHUSTER BOOKS FOR YOUNG READERS is a trademark of Simon & Schuster, Inc.
For information about special discounts for bulk purchases, please contact
Simon & Schuster Special Sales at 1-866-506-1949 or business@simonandschuster.com.
The Simon & Schuster Speakers Bureau can bring authors to your live event.
For more information or to book an event, contact the Simon & Schuster Speakers Bureau
at 1-866-248-3049 or visit our website at www.simonspeakers.com.
Book design by Laurent Linn
The text for this book is set in Joppa.
The illustrations for this book are rendered in Acryla gouache, applied with brayer, linocut, stamping, airbrush, sandpaper, and brush line.
Manufactured in China
1212 SCP
2 4 6 8 10 9 7 5 3 1
Library of Congress Cataloging-in-Publication Data
Johnson, Angela, 1961–
Lottie Paris and the best place / Angela Johnson ; illustrated by Scott M. Fischer. — 1st ed.
p. cm.
Summary: Lottie Paris goes to the library, her favorite place in the world, and makes a new friend for whom the library is also a special place.
ISBN 978-0-689-87378-2 (hardcover)
[1. Libraries—Fiction. 2. Friendship—Fiction.] I. Fischer, Scott M., ill. II. Title.
PZ7.J629Lov 2013
[E]—dc23
2011011303
ISBN 978-1-4424-3376-2 (eBook)

first edition

Lottie Paris

and the BEST PLACE

Angela Johnson

ILLUSTRATED BY

Scott M. Fischer

SIMON & SCHUSTER BOOKS FOR YOUNG READERS

New York   London   Toronto   Sydney   New Delhi

In the morning

Lottie Paris

wakes to stars that glow all around her

and to planets swiftly tilting from her ceiling.

She imagines herself floating among them.

And she **smiles**.

Now, here is Lottie Paris.

And this is Papa Pete walking her to the library.

Lottie runs ahead,

down the sidewalk

and up the library steps.

The library is Lottie's best place in the world.

But there are things
Lottie Paris knows about the library. . . .

You should **not** yell.

Dogs are **not** allowed.

And you **cannot** color—

inside **or** outside the lines.

Lottie Paris follows the rules, mostly. . . .

This is Carl.

He wakes up surrounded by dinosaurs.

He **imagines** them waiting

to walk him to the park.

And he **smiles**.

His sister, Eva,

is driving him to the **library**.

She listens to music

and to Carl talk about dinosaurs.

Carl hops
on one foot
up the library steps.

The library is **his** best place **too**.

And you **shouldn't** read books under the table and pretend everyone's feet are dinosaur snacks.

Carl follows those rules, sometimes.

Now, here is how Lottie Paris and Carl meet in the children's book room.

Lottie closes her eyes
and runs her hand down the shelf of books
about the planets and stars.

And on the other side of the shelf
Carl is doing the same, hoping the perfect
dinosaur book will
jump into his hand.

They **both** come to the ends of their shelves

and grab a book, open their eyes,

and **see** each other.

The librarian shakes her head at both of them, but smiles when she walks away.

Now, **here** are Lottie Paris and Carl sitting in the big,

yellow, plastic cheese chairs at the library.

And even though
they are **far away,**
dreaming among the planets and stars
and **running** with dinosaurs across field and swamp . . .

Lottie Paris and Carl will come back to the library **together** because now it is **their** best place in the world to be with **friends.**